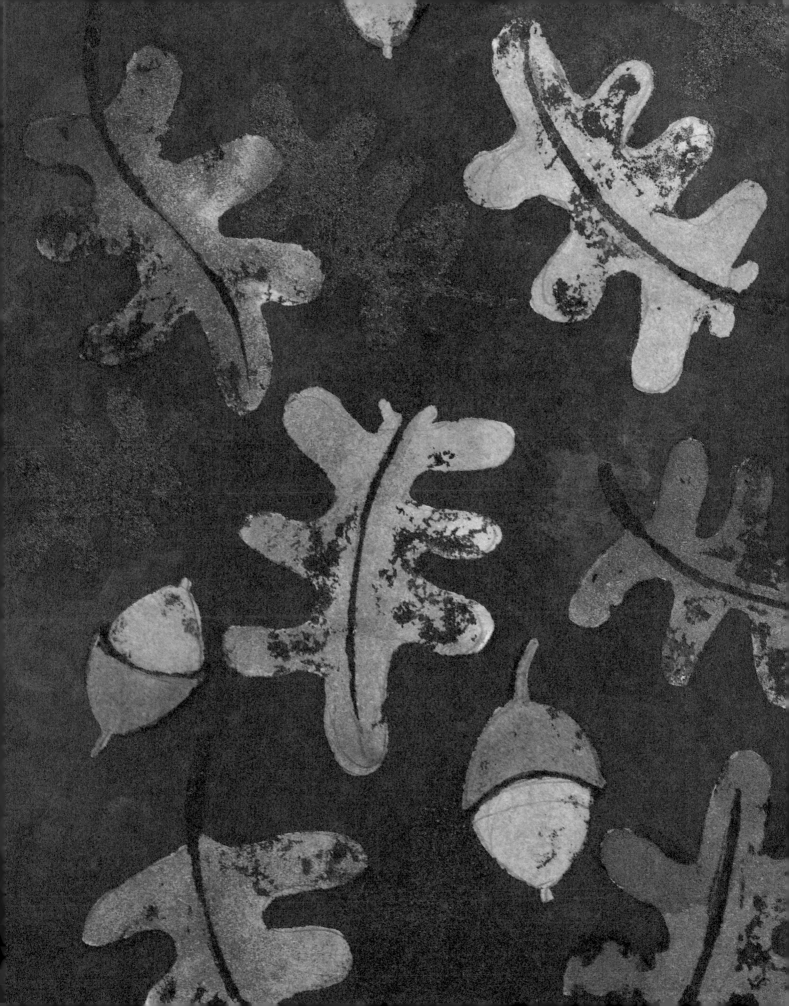

For Mum, Dad, and Jane, with love

SIMON & SCHUSTER BOOKS FOR YOUNG READERS

An imprint of Simon & Schuster Children's Publishing Division

1230 Avenue of the Americas

New York, New York 10020

Copyright © 1994 by Sally Hobson

SIMON & SCHUSTER BOOKS FOR YOUNG READERS

is a trademark of Simon & Schuster

Designed by Paul Zakris. The text for this

book is set in Goudy Sans Black

Reprinted by arrangement with Simon & Schuster Books for Young Readers,

Simon & Schuster Publishing Division.

Printed in USA   10 9 8 7 6 5 4 3 2

Library of Congress Catalog Card Number: 93-87521

Originally published in Great Britain by ABC,

All Books for Children, a division of

The All Children's Company Ltd.

First American Edition, 1994

ISBN: 0-671-89548-6

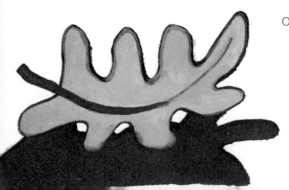

Chicken Little

Sally Hobson

SIMON & SCHUSTER
BOOKS FOR YOUNG READERS

One morning, an acorn fell
on Chicken Little's head. PLOP!

Chicken Little looked up.
"The sky is falling," he cheeped.
"I must tell the king."

"Hello," clucked Henny Penny.
"Where are you going in such a hurry?"
"The sky is falling," cheeped Chicken Little,
"and I must tell the king."
"Then I will trot with you,"
clucked Henny Penny.
So off they went.

And they went along,
   and they went along,
      and they went along.

"Hello," crowed Cocky Locky.
"Where are you going in such a hurry?"
"The sky is falling," cheeped Chicken Little,
"and we must tell the king."

"Then I will strut with you,"
crowed Cocky Locky.
So off they went.

And they went along,
and they went along,
and they went along.

"Hello," quacked Ducky Lucky.
"Where are you going in such a hurry?"
"The sky is falling," cheeped
Chicken Little, "and we
must tell the king."
"Then I will waddle with
you," quacked Ducky Lucky.
So off they went.

And they went along,
and they went along,
and they went along.

"Hello," gaggled Drakey Lakey.
"Where are you going in such a hurry?"

"The sky is falling," cheeped Chicken
Little, "and we must tell the king."
"Then I will toddle with you,"
gaggled Drakey Lakey.
So off they went.

And they went along,
and they went along,
and they went along.

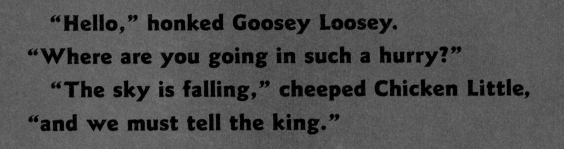

"Hello," honked Goosey Loosey.
"Where are you going in such a hurry?"
"The sky is falling," cheeped Chicken Little,
"and we must tell the king."

"Then I will jog with you,"
honked Goosey Loosey.
So off they went.

And they went along,
    and they went along,
        and they went along.

"Hello," gobbled Turkey Lurkey.
"Where are you going in such a hurry?"
"The sky is falling," cheeped Chicken Little,
"and we must tell the king."

"Then I will march with you," gobbled Turkey Lurkey. So off they went.

And they went along,
and they went along,
and they went along.

"The sky is falling," cheeped Chicken Little,
"and we must tell the king."
"Come with me," growled Foxy Loxy.
"I'll take you to the king."

So Chicken Little, Henny Penny, Cocky Locky,
Ducky Lucky, Drakey Lakey, Goosey Loosey,
and Turkey Lurkey followed Foxy Loxy straight
into his lair—and never came out again.

**And Chicken Little never told
the king the sky was falling.**

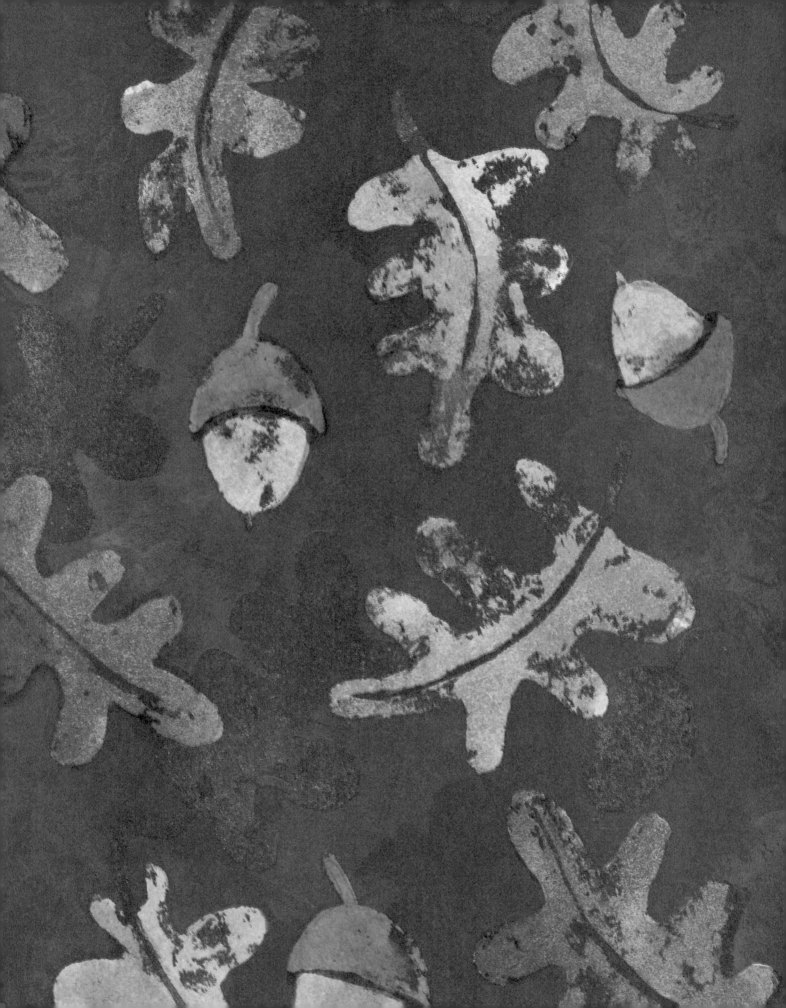